Goat in a boat

Lesley Sims

Illustrated by David Semple

"If I hook a fish, or two...

Cook can cook a fishy stew."

"I'll go for a row with Stoat," thinks Goat.

Stoat's room is bare.
There's no one there.

"Oh look! He wrote a note," says Goat.

Goat rows his boat around the moat.

He sits and gazes
at his float.

It sinks. He blinks.
"A fish!" he thinks.

He lifts his rod...

That's odd. It clinks.

Then Goat
spots Stoat.

Hop in
the boat!

They hear a noise among the trees.
Is it the breeze? The scared friends freeze.

An army!
Stoat has shaking knees.

But poor Stoat has a sore, sore throat.
He can't shout out along with Goat.

Then Goat hits on a clever plan.
They bash his catch...

CLASH! CLATTER! CLANG!

The lookout hears. He gives a cry.
The drawbridge rises to the sky.

The army
can't get in.
They flee.

Goat and Stoat
row home for tea.

Goat sighs. "I have no fish for Cook."

"You do," croaks Stoat.
"Just take a look!"

About phonics

Phonics is a method of teaching reading used extensively in today's schools. At its heart is an emphasis on identifying the *sounds* of letters, or combinations of letters, that are then put together to make words. These sounds are known as phonemes.

Starting to read
Learning to read is an important milestone for any child. The process can begin well before children start to learn letters and put them together to read words. The sooner children can discover books and enjoy stories and language, the better they will be prepared for reading themselves, first with the help of an adult and then independently.

You can find out more about phonics on the Usborne Very First Reading website, **www.usborne.com/veryfirstreading** (US readers go to **www.veryfirstreading.com**). Click on the **Parents** tab at the top of the page, then scroll down and click on **About synthetic phonics**.

Phonemic awareness

An important early stage in pre-reading and early reading is developing phonemic awareness: that is, listening out for the sounds within words. Rhymes, rhyming stories and alliteration are excellent ways of encouraging phonemic awareness.

In this story, your child will soon identify the *oa* sound, as in **goat** and **boat**. Look out, too, for rhymes such as **sinks** – **blinks** and **cry** – **sky**.

Hearing your child read

If your child is reading a story to you, don't rush to correct mistakes, but be ready to prompt or guide if he or she is struggling. Above all, do give plenty of praise and encouragement.

Edited by Jenny Tyler
Designed by Sam Whibley

Reading consultants: Alison Kelly and Anne Washtell

First published in 2015 by Usborne Publishing Ltd., Usborne House, 83-85 Saffron Hill, London EC1N 8RT, England.
www.usborne.com Copyright © 2015 Usborne Publishing Ltd.